CLASSIC FAIRY TALES

The
Sleeping
Beauty

Retold by Ann Turnbull

Illustrated by Sophy Williams

First published in Great Britain in 1997
by Macdonald Young Books
61 Western Road
Hove
East Sussex BN3 1JD

Text copyright © Ann Turnbull 1997
Illustrations copyright © Sophy Williams 1997

Designed by Shireen Nathoo Design

Typeset in 20pt Minion
Printed and bound in Belgium by Proost International Book Co.

British Library Cataloguing in Publication Data available.

ISBN: 0 7500 2001 6

One day in summer, a queen sat sewing beside a lake, and as she sewed her tears fell into the water.

A frog on a lily pad saw the tears and asked, "Queen, why do you weep?"

"Because I grow old and still I have no child," said the queen.

Then the frog said, "Dry your tears. Before a year is out you shall have a daughter."

And as the frog had promised, so it came to be. The queen gave birth to a baby daughter in the spring.

The king was overjoyed. He ordered a christening feast to be held, and sent messengers with invitations to every part of his kingdom. Knights, barons, earls, dukes and duchesses were invited, and the queen said, "We must not forget to invite the fairies."

There were thirteen fairies in the kingdom. Twelve of them were kind, but the thirteenth used her magic for evil. The king decided not to invite her.

On the day of the christening there were celebrations throughout the kingdom. Bells rang and flags flew, and the dancing and feasting went on for hours. The guests brought gifts for the baby: gold, emeralds, velvet, lace – every rich thing a princess could wish for.

When all the lords and ladies had given their gifts, the twelve fairies came forward with theirs. One gave the princess beauty; another grace. A third gave wisdom, a fourth, kindness; others, a voice like an angel, a light step in the dance, skill in playing every musical instrument.

Eleven fairies had given their gifts when a
shadow fell across the cradle. The thirteenth
fairy was there, and she was angry.

"You did not invite me to the christening,"
she said, "yet I have a gift for the child."

7

She leaned over the cradle: "When the princess is fifteen years old she will prick her finger on a spindle and die."

A cry of horror went around the hall. The queen fainted. The king begged forgiveness and implored the fairy to undo her spell, but she wrapped herself in her cloak and vanished.

"Can no one help us?" cried the king.

The twelfth fairy stepped forward. "I have not yet given my gift," she said.

The king turned to her in hope. "Will you break this spell?"

"No," said the fairy. "That is not in my power."

But she leaned over the cradle and said, "When the princess pricks her finger she shall not die, but sleep for a hundred years. A forest of thorns will grow up around the palace, and every living thing inside it will sleep until the day when a prince finds his way through the enchanted forest and wakes the princess with a kiss."

A hundred years! It seemed the same as death to the king. He ordered all spinning to be forbidden, all spindles burnt. If his daughter never saw a spindle, he thought, the fairy's curse could not come true.

The princess grew up as good and beautiful and clever as the fairies had promised, and everyone in the palace loved her.

On her fifteenth birthday a feast was to be held. In the kitchen the cooks simmered sauces and roasted meat; servants brought flowers and greenery to decorate the hall.

There was a whole room piled with gifts for the princess; there were letters from princes who hoped to win her hand in marriage.

The princess should have been excited.
The maids chattered as they combed her hair,
but the princess was quiet; she felt as if
something strange were about to happen to
her. When she was dressed she went to the
gallery and peeped down through a screen
into the great hall where guests were already
arriving and the musicians had begun to play.

"Leave me," she said to the maids. "I will go down alone."

When they had gone, she walked away from the hall, towards the older part of the palace where no one lived any more. She did not know her way around, yet she walked on with a firm step as if some will other than her own were drawing her. She came at last to the foot of a narrow, winding stairway.

The dust of years lay on the steps. She
walked up, leaving her footprints in the dust.

At the top was a door. She opened it and
went in.

She found herself in a little room where
an old woman stood twirling a spindle and
drawing out a length of woollen thread.

"Come in, my dear," said the old woman.
"I have been expecting you."

The princess did not know that the old woman was the thirteenth fairy in disguise. "What are you doing?" she asked.

"I am spinning," said the old woman. "Would you like to try?"

The princess took the spindle eagerly. But no sooner had she touched it than she pricked her finger and cried out.

Then the thirteenth fairy laughed in triumph, but the princess did not hear her; she had already fallen to the floor in a deep sleep.

At once, a change came over the palace. The maids in the gallery yawned, and lolled against the wall. The king and queen fell asleep on their thrones. The fiddler dropped his bow and the piper played a wailing note

as he slid to the floor. A cat creeping up on a mouse changed its mind, curled up, and went to sleep. The mouse slept; the horses in the stable slept; the doves in the dovecote slept. No leaf stirred; no breeze blew.

And now a forest began growing around the castle. Shoots sprang up, broke into leaf and put out thorns; branches thickened and lengthened. In an hour the palace walls were hidden; in a day the flag on the tower could not be seen. Month by month and year by year the forest grew, and the thorns locked together like chainmail so that no one could get in.

But the people remembered. They told of a hidden castle and a sleeping princess who could only be woken by a king's son. The story went around the land, and many princes came and tried to cut their way into the forest; but always the thorns caught and held them, and they died.

A hundred years passed by. On the last day of the fairy's spell a prince rode up with a company of hunters. They had been following a deer that led them far from home through woods and forests, through night and day, and brought them at last to the forest of thorns, where it vanished.

The people told the prince the story of the sleeping beauty. At once he knew that the deer had been sent to find him and that he was the one who must wake the princess.

"Leave this place. Go home," the people begged. They showed him the bones of long-dead princes caught in the thorns. But the prince was not afraid. He raised his sword and prepared to go in.

No sooner had the blade touched the first leaf than the entire forest broke into flower. The thorns parted, opening a way, and the scent of roses was all around. The prince sheathed his sword and stepped into the forest, and the thorns closed behind him.

He walked on through the blossoming forest until he reached the gates of the castle. The guards lay sleeping, their spears propped against the wall. He crossed the courtyard and came to an oak door studded with iron. He pushed it open and went into the great hall.

Before him, on two golden thrones, sat the king and queen, fast asleep. All around them, guests, servants and musicians lay sleeping on the floor. The prince stepped between  them and climbed the stairs to the gallery, where he found the maids asleep. He went on, towards the old part of the palace.

Through room after room he wandered, taking the same path that the princess had taken long ago. At last he came to the spiral staircase and there, in the dust, he saw her footprints. He followed them.

The door at the top was unlocked. He pushed it open and went inside.

On the floor lay the sleeping princess.
Her hair was as bright, her face as fresh as on
her fifteenth birthday a hundred years ago.
The prince, enchanted by her beauty, knelt
and kissed her.

At once the princess woke. She smiled, and sat up.

Below, in the hall, the king and queen stretched and rubbed their eyes. The guests began to stir. The cat woke; the mouse hid behind a chair.

The prince took the princess by the hand, and together they walked back through the empty rooms towards the great hall. As they drew nearer, they heard music and voices; they came upon the maids chattering behind the screen in the gallery; the hall was full of the scent of flowers, and light streamed in through the windows.

Outside the palace, the enchanted forest had disappeared, and with it the last of the fairy's magic. The king and queen welcomed the prince, and he declared his love for their daughter and asked for her hand in marriage. They agreed at once. And so the birthday feast that had begun a hundred years ago became a betrothal. The musicians struck up a lively tune, the dancing began, and all the bells rang out in celebration.

Other titles available in the Classic Fairy Tales series: